To all the best friends out there, starting with
Shane W. Evans, who first inspired this amazing journey.
Keep keeping each other honest and being there.
We all need each other. Much love and thanks.
—TD

Give gratitude to God, Light our path to friends.
Dedicated to ALL my family and friends,
big ups to my best Taye Diggs.
A "love shout out" to the team
that made this book real.
—SWE

A Feiwel and Friends Book
An imprint of Macmillan Publishing Group, LLC
120 Broadway, New York, NY 10271

Library of Congress Control Number: 2020911168
ISBN 978-1-250-13535-3 (hardcover)

Book design by Mallory Grigg
Feiwel and Friends logo designed by Filomena Tuosto

First edition, 2021
3 5 7 9 10 8 6 4 2
mackids.com

MY FRIEND!

WRITTEN BY
TAYE DIGGS

ILLUSTRATED BY
SHANE W. EVANS

Feiwel & Friends
New York

Rise and shine!
Time to climb out of bed!
Do what Daddy said.
Brush those teeth . . .

Slide without care
down those stairs.
Then dip, don't trip,
and sit right quick.

Shovel down that waffle
a bit, then split.

MY FRIEND!

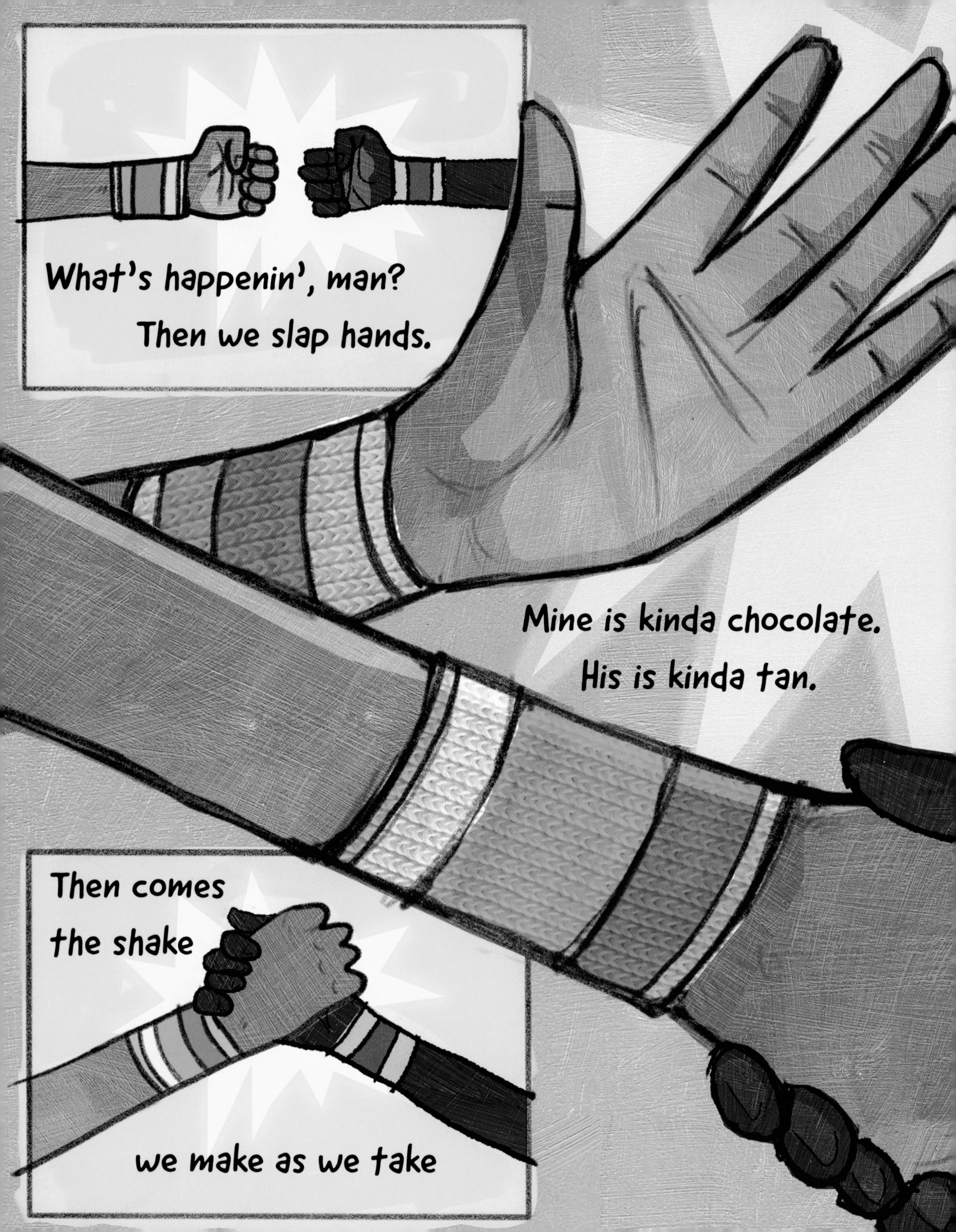
What's happenin', man?
Then we slap hands.
Mine is kinda chocolate.
His is kinda tan.
Then comes
the shake
we make as we take

Big smiles for miles,
walking down that aisle of the bus.
Must grab that seat just for US.
(The one cat I trust.)

Now! Let the fun begin.
Chattin' and laughin'
whispers and grins . . .

about today's game—who might lose, who might win.

MY FRIEND!

These are the things I go through
with you. My Crew.
'Cause you're . . .

MY FRIEND!

Jumpin' off the bus,
don't get crushed—
the opposite of hushed.

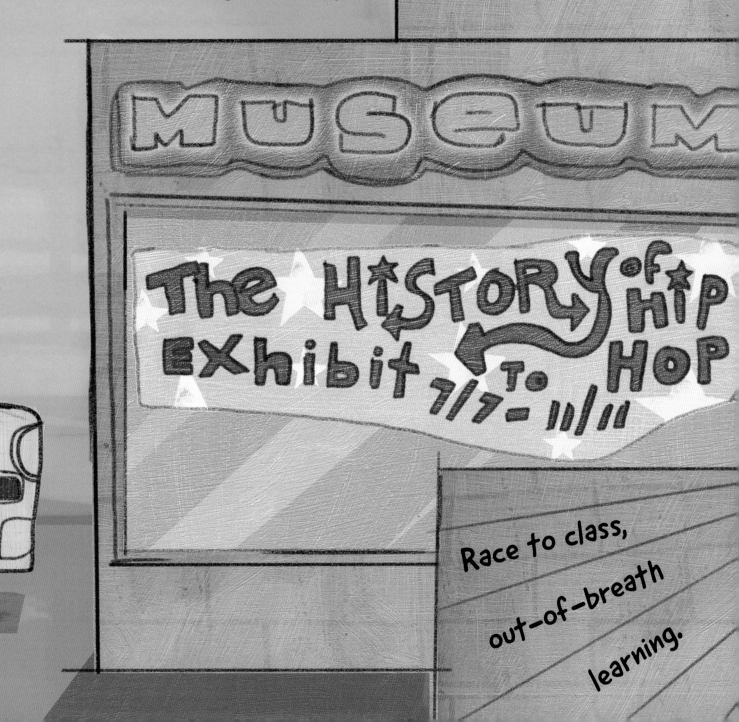

Kids shoving
and screaming,
even tag teaming.

MUSEUM

The HISTORY of hip
EXhibit to HOP
7/7 - 11/11

Race to class,
out-of-breath
learning.

Slamming into seats,
banging out beats
on desks,

rapping and
repeat,

using hands
and feet
until teacher
speaks,

while I compare
sneaks with . . .

Students' names are uttered.
The response: a muttered
"here" or "yup"
from all of the others.

Every name on the list,
not one child missed.
Attendance is done.
Are we dismissed?

Off to gym time—
      single-file line.

MY FRIEND in front while I fold in behind.
His duty is to lead; switching off the lights is mine.

              Off we march, keeping time.

But as I chill, since we had time to kill,
I spot MY FRIEND spilling ill will.
He sticks his leg out,
then comes a trip, then a shout,
then he points and laughs . . .
What's that about?

A kid's on the ground
with a pout.
I make up my mind
to change this route
'cause he's . . .

MY FRIEND.

I pull him aside and say,
"It's not cool when you act a fool.
Why trip somebody up and make fun?
That's not how this should be done.
Makes no sense, nuh-uh.
That's not how you treat someone."

MY FRIEND then slowly started to melt.
He seemed to feel a little of what I felt.

He took a
deep breath,
then knelt
and helped up
the fallen one,
apologized
for what
he'd done.

We brushed off his clothes
and continued to gym,
which is where he chose MY FRIEND
and me to be on his team.

The scene was like a buddy-buddy machine,
where we all work together.
Know what I mean?

love respect honor

hope faith

humor choice

family joy

Friends lend a hand when they can.
They help to blend and mend,
it doesn't depend on whether
you're doing wrong or right.

A friend can send or
lend a shining light
to a situation,
add some bright to
any frustration.

Looking after in any disaster,
come together and join in laughter,
arriving at a beautiful end
all because you're . . .

MY FRIEND.

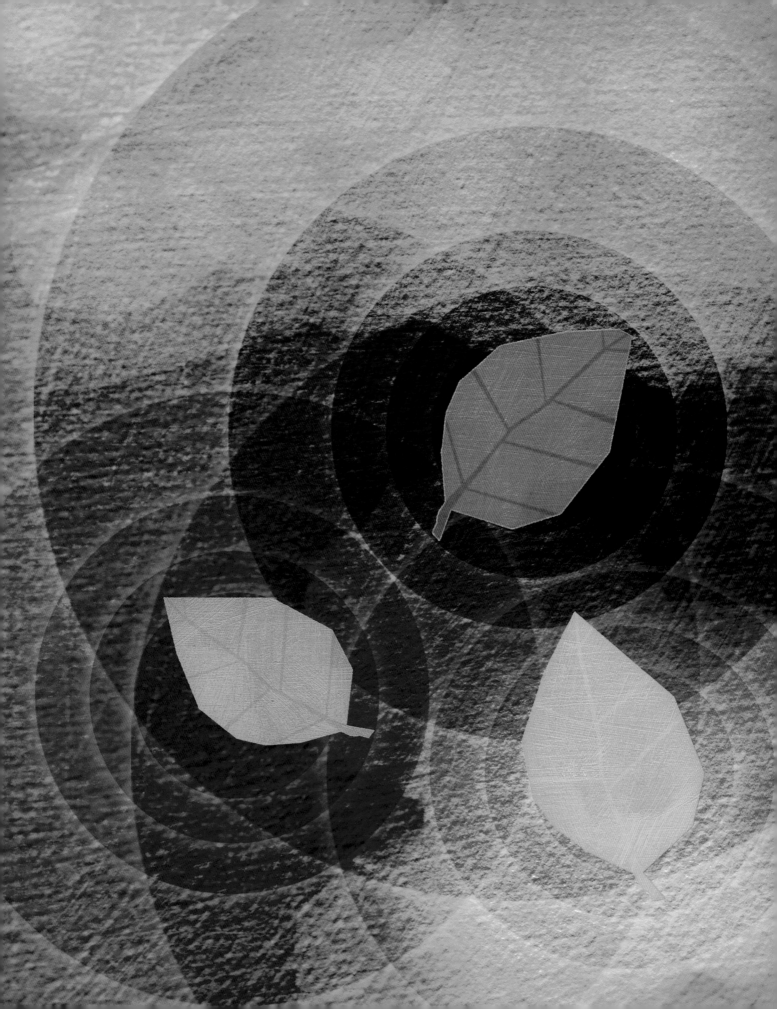

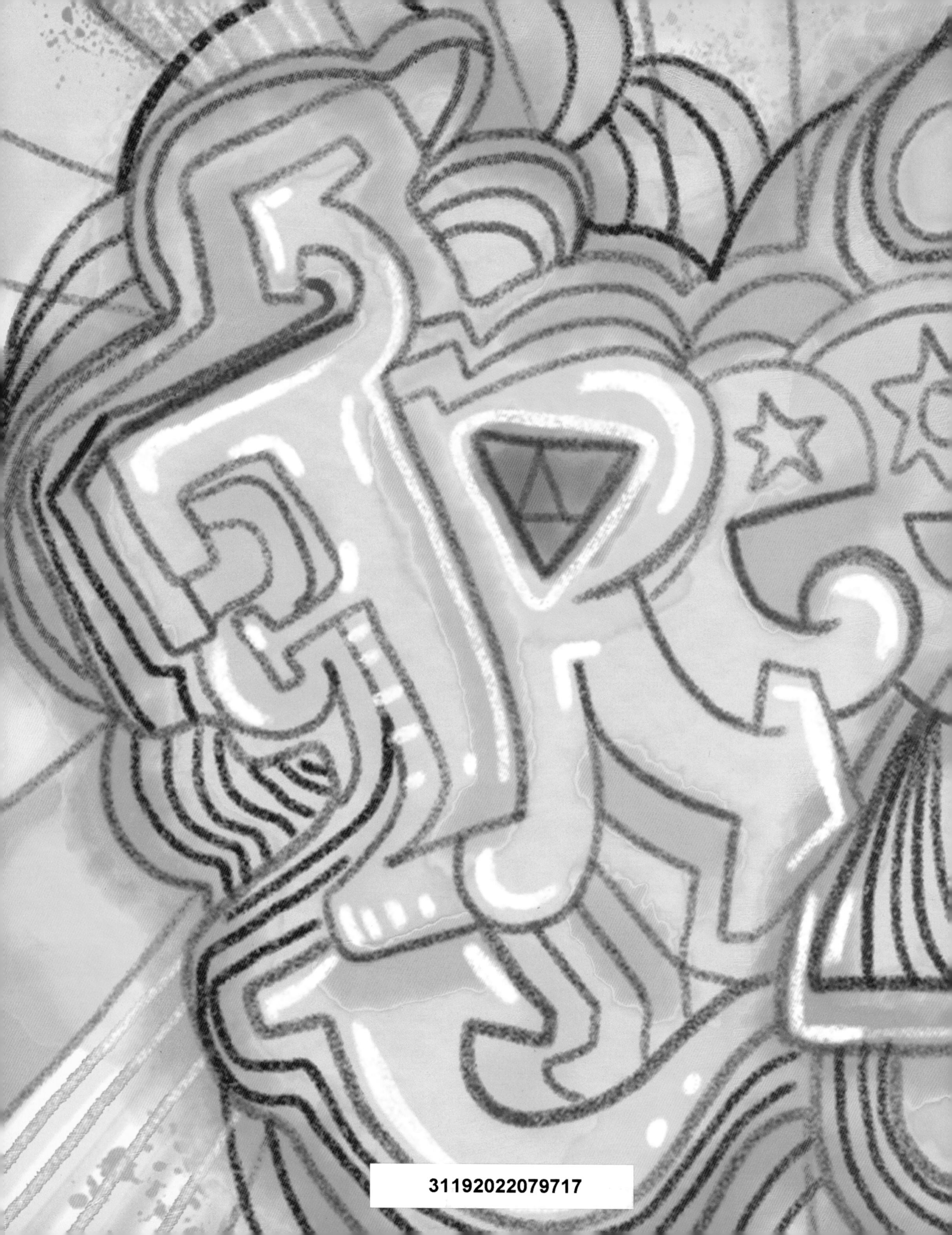